JONATHAN KEBBE

Illustrated by Sarah Nayler

www.randomhousechildrens.co.uk

SHREDDER
A CORGI BOOK 978 0 552 56898 2

Published in Great Britain by Corgi Books,
an imprint of Random House Children's Publishers UK
A Random House Group Company

Corgi Pups edition published 1998
This Colour First Reader edition published 2013

1 3 5 7 9 10 8 6 4 2

Copyright © Jonathan Kebbe, 2004
Illustrations copyright © Sarah Nayler, 2004

The Random House Group Limited supports the Forest Stewardship Council (FSC®),
the leading international forest certification organization. Our books carrying the FSC
label are printed on FSC®-certified paper. FSC is the only forest certification scheme
endorsed by the leading environmental organizations, including Greenpeace. Our paper
procurement policy can be found at www.randomhouse.co.uk/environment.

Set in Bembo MT Schoolbook 21/28pt

Corgi Books are published by Random House Children's Publishers UK,
61–63 Uxbridge Road, London W5 5SA

www.**randomhousechildrens**.co.uk
www.**totallyrandombooks**.co.uk
www.**randomhouse**.co.uk

Addresses for companies within The Random House Group Limited can be found at:
www.randomhouse.co.uk/offices.htm

THE RANDOM HOUSE GROUP Limited Reg. No. 954009

A CIP catalogue record for this book is available from the British Library.

Printed in Italy.

Contents

COLOUR FIRST READER books are perfect for beginner readers. All the text inside this Colour First Reader book has been checked and approved by a reading specialist, so it is the ideal size, length and level for children learning to read.

Series Reading Consultant: Prue Goodwin Honorary Fellow of the University of Reading

Chapter One

I'm Shredder, the class gerbil. I'm
furry and twitchy and tame. I'm
no bigger than a bar of soap,
and I live in a glass tank in Miss
Kimberly's classroom.

I'm called Shredder because that's what I do. I shred paper and cardboard with my tiny teeth, filling my home with soft litter. Look closely and you'll see all the tunnels I've made in the litter, and a cosy little nest in the corner.

nest

It gets lonely sometimes. Every morning I run around, hoping to meet another gerbil but I never do. I get scared too, because Mr Blister, the new headteacher, doesn't like me.

He came in this morning and said to Miss Kimberly, "I wish you'd get rid of that nasty little creature."

Nasty? I'm not nasty.

"Oh I couldn't do that, Mr Blister," whispered Miss Kimberly, who is small and plump and terribly nervous. "The children would be so upset."

"Upset? Nonsense!" said Mr Blister, turning to face the class. All the children  shrank in their seats, because Mr Blister looked like the giant in *Jack and the Beanstalk.*

"I like a nice, clean school,"
he said, smiling sweetly. "And
classroom pets are smelly and
dirty. This one certainly is," he
sniffed.

"Sir, sir, sir!" A boy's hand shot up! It was Dino, a funny, long-haired boy, who's always bringing me seeds to eat. He spends ages standing watching me. He's loud and a little crazy,  and no one plays with him much. I'm his only friend. And now his hand was up.

"You're wrong, sir," he cried.

"Wrong?" boomed Mr Blister.

"Yes, sir!" said Dino. "Shredder's not dirty, he's very clean."

"Clean?"

"He's a desert rat, sir. Desert

12

rats don't need much water, so they hardly ever pee!"

Everyone looked at Dino, amazed.

Mr Blister went off shaking

his head and mumbling, "Most peculiar children."

A few minutes later he marched out into the school

garden wearing his wellies and wielding a spade. Whenever he's angry, he digs the heavy soil until the sweat runs down his face. Mr Blister *loves* his garden. It's his favourite place in the whole school.

Phew! I sighed, wiggling my whiskers. I'm safe . . . for the moment.

"Well said, Dino!" cried Miss Kimberly. "You're a brave boy."

"A nutter, miss!" someone said.

Children laughed, but Dino wanted to ask a question.

"Miss, does that mean I can take Shredder out and play with him now?"

"Goodness me, no!"

"But, miss—"

"Dino, I keep telling you – if Shredder escaped, Mr Blister would have a fit! We must be very careful. Never take him out on your own again. Is that understood?"

"Yes, miss."

Miss Kimberly returned to her desk.

"Look, children! Remember
all those 20ps and 50ps and
pound coins you brought in for
our seaside trip? Well, I took the
bag of coins to the bank, and
they exchanged them for ten
crisp new ten-pound notes. So
now we have ten pounds times
ten. And what does that add
up to?"

"A million!" cried Dino.
Everybody laughed. Hands

shot up. "One hundred pounds, miss!"

"Yes! One hundred pounds!" she announced, waving the crisp new notes in the air. "More than enough for a wonderful day out."

Everyone was excited, painting pictures of sand castles and sailboats, and the fairground they were going to visit.

Only Dino painted something different — a big picture of *me* shredding a HUGE cornflakes box.

"In a minute I want one of you to take the money to Mr Blister, so he can lock it safely away," said Miss Kimberly.

"Me, miss!" children cried.

But Miss Kimberly chose Dino, because it was break time, and Dino gets lonely at break times. Everyone ran out to play.

"Oh dear, I can't find my envelopes," sighed Miss Kimberly.

 "You'll just have to take the money in this," she said, and carefully placed the ten ten-pound notes inside a nearly empty tissue box.

"Miss, first I've got to change Shredder's water," said Dino.

"No, you can't stay alone in here."

"It won't take a sec, miss."

"You can do it later."

"But, miss, his water's disgusting. You *told* us. He has to have fresh water every single day."

"All right, but quickly. I'll leave the money in my desk. Change Shredder's water, take the money to Mr Blister and then find me in the playground."

Miss Kimberly put the tissue box in the top drawer of her desk, and carefully closed it.

Chapter Two

As soon as Miss Kimberly had
gone, Dino lifted the lid on
my tank, unclipped my water
bottle and replaced the lid so
I couldn't escape. He emptied
the stale water and refilled it.

Then he opened the lid on my
tank and replaced the bottle.
The lid was still open. Dino was
looking at me.

"It's not right she won't let me
take you out on my own any
more, Shredder," he said.

He looked out the window. Mr Blister had finished digging and was returning indoors. Miss Kimberly was supervising children in the playground.

I tried to yell – "*Don't do it, Dino! You'll get in trouble.*" But he couldn't hear me. He lifted me out of the tank and rubbed his nose against mine.

"*Shhh*, we don't want to get caught!" he whispered, which was funny, because I didn't make any noise. I only squeak when I get a fright.

He had me on his shoulder. I ran down his arm, over his head,

and down the other arm. Up his sleeve I went, and inside his sweater,

making Dino laugh.
Then I was nibbling
his school tie. I
love shredding
ties. Then he let
me chase a ping-pong ball on
Miss Kimberly's desk.

What fun we were having ...
until suddenly – someone was
coming!

Squeak! Hide!

It was Miss Kimberly.

"Dino, what's going on?"

"Nothing, miss."

"Are you sure?"

Looking round the room, her eyes fell on my tank. The open lid!

"Where is he?"

"Who, miss?"

"You know who!"

"Um . . . I don't know, miss."

Miss Kimberly looked *very* worried.

"You didn't take him out, Dino, did you?"

Dino lowered his eyes.

"Dino, I'm talking to you. Did you?"

"Yes, miss."

"Well, where is he then?"

"He's . . . he's . . . gone, miss!"

It was true. Miss Kimberly hadn't fully shut the top drawer of her desk, and I squeezed inside. It was nice and dark in there. Even cosier inside the tissue box.

Oh dear, what's happening? Miss Kimberly was running out and calling, "Quickly, children. Shredder's escaped!"

Chapter Three

Clatter-clatter-clatter.

Everyone was running in to look for me.

Squeak-squeak! The fuss was frightening. And when I'm frightened, I grab any paper I find and start shredding – *nip-nip-nip-nip-nip!* I can't help it.

I started to shred the crisp sheets
of paper in the tissue box, and
made myself a nice little nest
of shredded ten-pound notes.
The few remaining tissues neatly
hid me.

Who's that? Heavy footfalls!
Mr Blister!

"What's going on in here, Miss
Kimberly? Why are your children
crawling round on their hands
and knees?"

Squeak-squeak! My heart was going to explode!

"They're, um, picking up any bits of paper they can find," replied Miss Kimberly.

"They look as if they're looking for something."

"No! They're not looking for anything."

"We're just very tidy kids, sir!" said Dino.

"Good. That's what I like to hear," said Mr Blister. "I do like a nice, clean school."

He marched out again.

Phew! I was safe again. Or was I?

The search went on. But they still couldn't find me.

"He must have jumped out of the window, miss!" someone called.

I could hear Miss Kimberly telling Dino off. "I told you not to take him out, and now look what you've done!"

The other children were angry too.

"You've lost Shredder, you fool, Dino."

"He'll die out there."

"A cat will get him."

"He'll be run over."

Dino didn't answer. Miss Kimberly made everyone work in silence. I lay absolutely still in my new nest. My sharp ears picked up the sound of a boy softly crying.

"Miss," someone called. "Dino's crying."

"What's the matter, Dino?"

"Shredder, miss . . . I only wanted to stroke him and give him a bit of fun. Every animal needs a bit of love. And now he's going to die and it's all my fault."

Miss Kimberly tried to comfort him, but Dino couldn't stop crying.

I must climb out and show myself, I was thinking, *before poor Dino breaks his heart.* But just as I was about to get out of the box, Miss Kimberly said, "Dino, would you like to take the money down to the office?"

_Sniff

"No, I don't care about the money. I'm never going to the seaside, or anywhere, ever again."

"*You* may not care, Dino," said Miss Kimberly, opening the drawer of her  desk, "but everyone else is really looking forward to it. Work quietly, everyone. I won't be a minute. I'll leave the classroom door open and just be up the corridor."

Whoops! Lie low! I thought, as the tissue box was lifted out of the drawer with me trembling inside it.

Miss Kimberly carried it out of
the room and down the corridor.
Through a gap in the box, I saw
a door marked HEADTEACHER'S
OFFICE. *Oh no!*

Knock-knock.
"Come in!"
There he was. The giant!
Seated at his desk. He was the
last person I wanted to see!

"Sorry to disturb you, Mr
Blister. This is my seaside trip
money. One hundred pounds.
I'm sorry I couldn't find an
envelope."

"A tissue box! Ah well. As long as the money is safe."

I could feel the box bump down onto the desk. I could hear Miss Kimberly leaving. *What do I do now?*

Whoops! I was flying again. Mr Blister had picked up the box.

"Better lock this money away," he muttered to himself. The next thing I saw was a big hairy hand reaching under the top layer of tissues to grab me.

I was out in bright light again, trapped in the giant's hand, trying to flatten myself out like a ten-pound note. But Mr Blister stopped suddenly and stared

at what was in his hand. Not
money – but a desert rat!

"*Ahhhhhhhhhh!*" he
screamed, and threw me into
the air. I hit the ceiling . . . and
then the floor. *Ouch!* My head!
Ouch! My paws!

Quick – *Squeak-squeak!* I was up the table leg and out through the open window!

"Miss Kimberly," yelled Mr Blister. "*MISS KIMBERLY!*"

Chapter Four

My head was still sore. My
heart was sorer still. I hid in the
garden, never stirring except
to hunt for seeds. I didn't mind
being outside, but I missed my
tank. Now I was missing the

children, especially Dino. It had been such fun playing with him. It felt so good when he stroked me.

Climbing up onto the window ledge, I sneaked a look into the classroom as the children arrived back after lunch.

Each girl and boy went straight to my tank, hoping by some miracle I was back. Everyone was upset. Dino's eyes were full of tears.

Mr Blister entered the room. He was holding the tissue box and looking *very* stern. Miss Kimberly was looking *very* nervous. Mr Blister emptied the box onto her desk. The shredded ten-pound notes spilled out in a heap. Goodness me, did I do that?

"Please restore this money to its former glory, Miss Kimberly," he said, glaring at the class. "Let that be a lesson to you. Never keep nasty animals!"

He walked out again. Miss Kimberly called Dino up to the front. She was searching in her desk, saying "I'm sure I had some sticky tape here somewhere."

At afternoon break, I sneaked a look in the staffroom window. Miss Kimberly had ALL the teachers taping scraps of money back together.

At the end of the day I watched the children pack up quietly and go home.

The night set in. I sat very still among Mr Blister's flowers, watching cats and cars come and go. It was no good. I had to do something. I couldn't bear to see Dino's sad face again. Either I left and took my chances with the cats and cars, or . . .

Chapter Five

It was easy stealing back into
the school in the dead of night.
It was harder climbing back into
the tank. Luckily, when I dashed
under the classroom door and
up the table leg, I found that
the lid of my tank had been

carelessly replaced, leaving a
squeezing-in gap.

In the morning, when the
children arrived, I crawled out
of my tunnels and stood up on
my hind legs to see who would
come in first.

Guess who it was! Dino! He'd
come in before the teacher. He
looked so sad as he dropped his
bag on his chair and came over
to the tank. He was looking

straight at me. Blinked. Looked
away. He couldn't believe
it. Looked at me again. His
mouth fell open.

He reached over very slowly,
lifted the lid. I was in his hands
again. He was rubbing my
fur gently against his cheek.

Footsteps in the corridor. A grown-up's footsteps. I felt Dino's hands tighten around my bony body.

"What are you doing in here, Dino? And what have you got there?"

Dino turned slowly.

"A gerbil?" said Miss Kimberly. "You've got a new one?"

"No, miss. It's Shredder."

"You found him!"

"No, miss. He came back by himself. He *loves* it here."

A shadow fell across the room. Mr Blister! He stared at me.

"I *was* about to deliver some good news," he said. "The bank  has kindly agreed to replace the patched-up notes with new ones."

The other children were coming in now. They looked at Mr Blister. They saw Dino holding me and whispered to each other.

"Is it a new gerbil?"

"No, it's Shredder. He's come back."

Children were moving carefully round Mr Blister, coming to make sure it really

was me. They all looked at each other.

Mr Blister took a huge step towards us. Everyone froze.

"After that creature shredded up all your money, I'm surprised you children still want to keep him. What use is he?"

Dino looked up at him.
"Sir! Guess what? My dad says shredded paper is good for compost heaps, and what your garden needs is a compost heap. Just think of all the waste paper and cardboard Shredder could shred for you. Shredder's not a pest, sir. He's a hard worker. And guess what, sir? We wouldn't charge you a penny!"

Mr Blister's eyebrows swooped like eagles. Was he going to go mad?

No! A smile broke across his face.

"*Hmmm*," he rumbled, rubbing his chin. "I'll have to think about it."

After he had gone, Miss Kimberly gave Dino *two* excited thumbs up!

Dino kissed me, and everyone crowded round to stroke me.

"Welcome back, Shredder"

They slapped Dino on the back.

"Well done, Dino, you're brilliant!"

Miss Kimberly tapped her desk. "Come on, children. Books out."

With a HUGE HAPPY SMILE Dino put me back in my tank.

I'm home.

THE END

Colour First Readers

Welcome to Colour First Readers. The following pages are intended for any adults (parents, relatives, teachers) who may buy these books to share the stories with youngsters. The pages explain a little about the different stages of learning to read and offer some suggestions about how best to support children at a very important point in their reading development.

Children start to learn about reading as soon as someone reads a book aloud to them when they are babies. Book-loving babies grow into toddlers who enjoy sitting on a lap listening to a story, looking at pictures or joining in with familiar words. Young children who have listened to stories start school with an expectation of enjoyment from books and this positive outlook helps as they are taught to read in the more formal context of school.

Cracking the code

Before they can enjoy reading for and to themselves, all children have to learn how to crack the alphabetic code and make meaning out of the lines and squiggles we call letters and punctuation. Some lucky pupils find the process of learning to read undemanding; some find it very hard.

Most children, within two or three years, become confident at working out what is written on the page. During this time they will probably read collections of books which are graded; that is, the books introduce a few new words and increase in length, thus helping youngsters gradually to build up their growing ability to work out the words and understand basic meanings.

Eventually, children will reach a crucial point when, without any extra help, they can decode words in an entire book, albeit a short one. They then enter the next phase of becoming a reader.

Making meaning

It is essential, at this point, that children stop seeing progress as gradually 'climbing a ladder' of books of ever-increasing difficulty. There is a transition stage between building word recognition skills and enjoying reading a story. Up until now, success has depended on getting the words right but to get pleasure from reading to themselves, children need to fully comprehend the content of what they read. Comprehension will only be reached if focus is put on understanding meaning and that can only happen if the reader is not hesitant when decoding. At this fragile, transition stage, decoding should be so easy that it slowly becomes automatic. Reading a book with ease enables children to get lost in the story, to enjoy the unfolding narrative at the same time as perfecting their newly learned word recognition skills.

At this stage in their reading development, children need to:

- Practice their newly established early decoding skills at a level which eventually enables them to do it automatically

- Concentrate on making sensible meanings from the words they decode

- Develop their ability to understand when meanings are 'between the lines' and other use of literary language

- Be introduced, very gradually, to longer books in order to build up stamina as readers

In other words, new readers need books that are well within their reading ability and that offer easy encounters with humour, inference, plot-twists etc. In the past, there have been very few children's books that provided children with these vital experiences at an early stage. Indeed, some children had to leap from highly controlled teaching materials to junior novels.

This experience often led to reluctance in youngsters who were not yet confident enough to tackle longer books.

Matching the books to reading development

Colour First Readers fill the gap between early reading and children's literature and, in doing so, support inexperienced readers at a vital time in their reading development. Reading aloud to children continues to be very important even after children have learned to read and, as they are well written by popular children's authors, Colour First Readers are great to read aloud. The stories provide plenty of opportunities for adults to demonstrate different voices or expression and, in a short time, give lots to talk about and enjoy together.

Each book in the series combines a number of highly beneficial features, including:

- Well-written and enjoyable stories by popular children's authors

- Unthreatening amounts of print on a page

- Unrestricted but accessible vocabularies

- A wide interest age to suit the different ages at which children might reach the transition stage of reading development

- Different sorts of stories – traditional, set in the past, present or future, real life and fantasy, comic and serious, adventures, mysteries etc.

- A range of engaging illustrations by different illustrators

- Stories which are as good to read aloud to children as they are to be read alone

All in all, Colour First Readers are to be welcomed for children throughout the early primary school years – not only for learning to read but also as a series of good stories to be shared by everyone. I like to think that the word 'Readers' in the title of this series refers to the many young children who will enjoy these books on their journey to becoming lifelong bookworms.

Prue Goodwin
Honorary Fellow of the University of Reading

Helping children to enjoy *Shredder*

If a child can read a page or two fluently, without struggling with the words at all, then he/she should be able to read this book alone. However, children are all different and need different levels of support to help them become confident enough to read a book to themselves.

Some young readers will not need any help to get going; they can just get on with enjoying the story. Others may lack confidence and need help getting into the story. For these children, it may help if you talk about what might happen in the book.

Explore the title, cover and first few illustrations with them, making comments about any clues to what might happen in the story. Read the first chapter aloud together. Don't make it a chore. If they are still reluctant to read alone, share the whole book with them, making it an enjoyable experience.

The following suggestions will not be necessary every time a book is read but, every so often, when a story has been particularly enjoyed, children love responding to it through creative activities.

Before reading

Who is telling this story? It makes a difference when we know who the narrator is. In this case it's a gerbil who tells a tale from his specific point of view, so we only hear his version of events. Talk briefly about how Shredder might feel about being a class pet.

During reading

Asking questions about a story can be really helpful to support understanding but don't ask too many – and don't make it into a test on what happens. Relate the questions to the child's own experiences and imagination. For example, ask: 'Is this school like yours?'; and 'Do you have a class pet?' Perhaps comment on the human characters but remember we only have Shredder's descriptions to help us. Is Miss Kimberly a nice teacher? Mr Blister seems very grumpy; does he like anything? What do we think about Dino's personality?

Responding to the book

If your child has enjoyed the story, it increases the fun by doing something creative in response. If possible, provide art materials and dressing-up clothes so that they can make things, play at being characters, act out a scene or respond in some other way to the story.

Activities for children

If you have enjoyed reading this story, you could:

• Look up gerbils (also called desert rats) on the Internet to find out more about them.

• Share the story with your friends and, using the different characters, act out the classroom scene in Chapter One.

• Get a piece of paper and a pen to write down Shredder's journey. Where did Shredder go next?

Reread the story to put the places in the right order:

Shredder went from his cage to ...

1. a tissue box then . . .

2. Dino's hands . . .

3. the headteacher's office . . .

4. Miss Kimberly's desk drawer . . .

. . . into the garden.

• Answer True or False:

1. Gerbils like to chew up bits of paper
   T or F

2. Shredder ran away from the school
   T or F

3. Shredded paper makes good compost
   for the garden   T or F

4. The class trip was cancelled   T or F

5. Dino wanted to care for Shredder   T or F